Mouse Tail Moon

Joanne Ryder

illustrated by

Maggie Kneen

Henry Holt and Company

New York

Henry Holt and Company, LLC
Publishers since 1866
115 West 18th Street
New York, New York 10011
www.henryholt.com

Library of Congress Cataloging-in-Publication Data
Ryder, Joanne.
Mouse tail moon / by Joanne Ryder; illustrated by Maggie Kneen.
Summary: A series of poems that depict the world of a field mouse from sundown to sunup.
1. Mice—Juvenile poetry. 2. Children's poetry, American. [1. Mice—Poetry.
2. American poetry.]   I. Kneen, Maggie, ill. II. Title.
PS3568.Y399 M68 2002   811'.54—dc21   2001004508

ISBN 0-8050-6404-4 / First Edition—2002
Designed by Martha Rago
The artist used watercolor on hot-pressed watercolor paper
to create the illustrations for this book.
Printed in the United States of America on acid-free paper. ∞
1   3   5   7   9   10   8   6   4   2

A Note to the Reader

These are the poems of a white-footed mouse, a creature of the dusk and night. They reflect its view of mouse life and its world—though even a small poet takes some licenses. You might find such a mouse in many places throughout the countryside.

The poems are gathered to reveal one night from sunset to sunrise. On this night, an early evening moon is just a bright sliver, looking like a slender tail high in the sky.

Welcome to the night of the Mouse Tail Moon as someone small stirs, someone aware and watchful, someone lively—a poet wrapped in silky fur.

Joanne Ryder

Sunberry

Like a berry
ripe and round,
sun slips,
dipping down,
spilling
RED RED RED—
Oh, my!
at the bottom
of the sky.

Mouse Tail Moon

There's a sliver of moon
like a tail in the sky
with just enough moonlight
to make my way by.
There are seeds in the grass,
and nuts on the ground,
and berries just waiting
to be sniffed, to be found.
Owl won't see me—
it isn't that bright.
But the Mouse Tail Moon
guides me through the dusk,
through the night.

Darkness Is My Friend

Darkness is my friend.
No one sees me.
Darkness is my friend.
I am small.
In the night I know
darkness hides me,
and I feel much braver and tall.
All around, I hear others like me.
We are those
who darkness sets free.
We are those
who rustle and whisper,
living lives outsiders won't see.
We are born and die
in the darkness,
sharing comfort shadows can lend—
melting in the
brightness of daylight
when the nighttime
comes to its end.
In the dark
I too am a shadow.
Darkness is my friend.

A Chant for Protection
(against Fox, Cat, and Owl)

May my Eyes see thee
before thee sees me.
May my Nose smell thee
before thee smells me.
May my Ears hear thee
before thee hears me.
And may seeds fill me—
but not *me* fill thee.

The Chase

Claws out,
beak wide,
owl plunges.
Can I hide?
Ears high,
nose down,
paws racing
over ground.
Turn left.
Spin right.
Look! A hole—
snug and tight.
Claws fail.
Paws win.
He's out.
I'm in!

Sniffing

This is a path
that another mouse took.
I can smell
his damp footprints
where he stopped.
And look . . .
here are some
grass seeds.
I'm sure he
won't mind
if I nibble the
ones that have
fallen behind.

Tasty Advice

A taste of this and that is nice.
The world's a grand buffet for mice.
With teeth as sharp as teeth should be,
you're free to sample what you see.
No need to finish what you start—
just have a nip and then depart.
Yet count your snacks or you'll get fat,
and end up supper for a cat!

Whisker Wise

It doesn't matter
what your size.
You're smart
if you are whisker wise.
Just spread each whisker
round your face
to judge the crack,
the gap,
the space.
If whiskers bend
you're out of luck.
Don't go!
Pull back!
You might get stuck.

We clever mice
heed this advice
and so do rats
and even . . .
CATS!

Fleas

They do not
say, *"Hello."*
They do not
say, *"Nice day."*
Like night
they come,
without a word.
I wish they'd
stay away.
They hide
within my fur.
Six feet creep
on my skin.
They bite
and bite
and hold on tight
like pricking,
sticking pins.
They're small,
but oh, they nibble so.
Please, please, fat fleas,
skedaddle! GO!

Shower

Rain
plops
on a leaf.
I hide
underneath.
Drops
sink
in the
ground.
Mud
paints
pale paws
brown.
Wind blows.
Clouds fly.
Rain stops.
I'm dry.

Good-bye, Spiders!

The tall grass
is hung
with a garland of lace.
Spiders are spinning
and leaping toward space.
Spiderlings soar,
and I wish I could too,
as I stand under streamers
beaded with dew.
On a whisper of wind,
spiders take to the sky
to places unknown.
Happy journeys!
Good-bye!

Night Path

A dark gray blur
in a world of gray,
a night one races
feeling her way,
touching stone
smooth and steep
to a jagged spur
where she leaps . . .
riding air
to the branch
that is there
always waiting
for her.

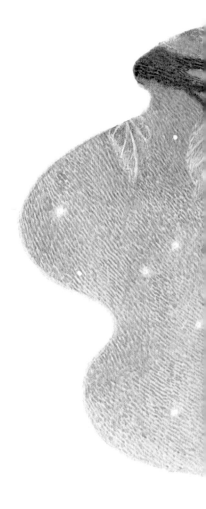

Brother

Last night
a mouse ran
up the hill,
alive and leaping,
and then stood still
to feel
the rushing wind
brush fur
against his skin.
He didn't hear
fox creeping.

Tonight
the field has
one less mouse.
How easy
to dismiss him.
But I am sad
to see him go.
The grass sighs,
empty now,
and oh . . .
I miss him.

Listen!

Small paws
drumming
on a fallen tree
passing
secrets
from
mouse
to me.
I drum
my message
in the dawn:
Day is
coming.
Pass it on.

Bright Treasures

Branches
stretching
overhead
dangle berries
eat me red.
Branches
drooping
on the ground
bring me breakfast
sweet and round.

Dancing Mice

As the
morning sun
touches
and tickles
my skin,
I feel
like a top
that is
ready to spin.
It's hard
to know why
I twirl
like a toy,
but I know
that we mice
just dance
for the joy—
of being
mice.

Mousekin

Mama mice,
baby mice
curl in their beds—
fat balls
of tummies
and whiskers
and heads.
A nest
full of mice
is as nice
as can be
and the
very best
home
for a mousekin
like me.

A Mousekin Blessing

From the tip of my nose
to the tip of my tail,
I wish you a day
fair and warm.
May wonders be many
and troubles be few
as you roam
through the world
safe from harm.
And when the day's over,
please wish me the same,
as you rest
and I breathe the night air.
From the tip of my nose
to the tip of my tail,
may we treasure
this world that we share.